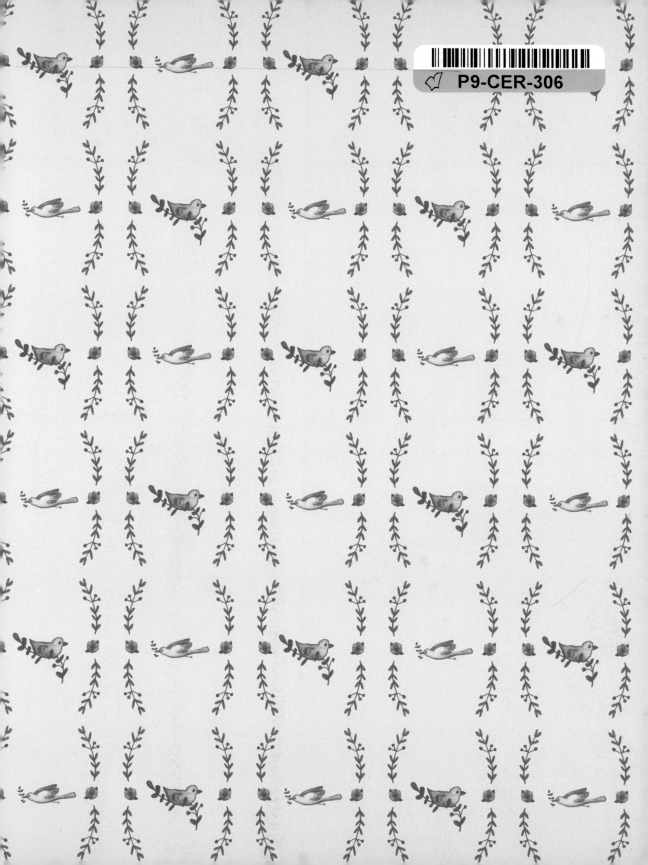

Peace
is an

La paz es una

Words by
Annette LeBox

Palabras de Annette LeBox

Dial Books for Young Readers
an imprint of Penguin Group (USA) LLC

Offering
Ofrenda

pictures by
Stephanie Graegin

Dibujos de
Stephanie Graegin

Traducción de Teresa Mlawer

For Charly, hugs —ALB   *A Charly, abrazos –ALB*

For my siblings —SG   *A mis hermanos –SG*

DIAL BOOKS FOR YOUNG READERS
Published by the Penguin Group
Penguin Group (USA) LLC
375 Hudson Street
New York, New York 10014

USA / Canada / UK / Ireland / Australia / New Zealand / India / South Africa / China
penguin.com
A Penguin Random House Company

Text copyright © 2015 by Annette LeBox
Pictures copyright © 2015 by Stephanie Graegin

Library of Congress Cataloging-in-Publication Data
LeBox, Annette.
Peace is an offering / words by Annette LeBox ; pictures by Stephanie Graegin.
pages cm
Summary: Illustrations and simple, rhyming text show different ways that peace can be found, made, and shared.
ISBN 9780803740914 (hardcover)
Special Markets ISBN: 9780399186707 Not for Resale
[1. Stories in rhyme. 2. Peace—Fiction.] I. Graegin, Stephanie, illustrator. II. Title.
PZ8.3.L484Pe 2015 [E]—dc23 2013050557

Manufactured in China on acid-free paper

1 3 5 7 9 10 8 6 4 2

Designed by Lily Malcom • Text set in Fiesole

The illustrations were rendered in pencil and watercolor and then assembled and colored digitally.

This Imagination Library edition is published by Penguin Young Readers, a division of Penguin Random House, exclusively for Dolly Parton's Imagination Library, a not-for-profit program designed to inspire a love of reading and learning, sponsored in part by The Dollywood Foundation. Penguin's trade editions of this work are available wherever books are sold.

Peace is an offering.
A muffin or a peach.

La paz es una ofrenda.
Un dulce o melocotón.

A birthday invitation.

Una fiesta de cumpleaños.

A trip to the beach.

A la playa de excursión.

Peace is gratitude for simple things.

Paz es dar las gracias por todas las cosas.

Light through a leaf, a dragonfly's wings.

Alas de libélula, luz entre las hojas.

A kiss on the head, raindrops and dew.
A walk in the park, a bowl of hot stew.

Un beso en la cabeza, gotas de lluvia y relente.
Un paseo por el parque, un buen guiso caliente.

Peace is holding on to another.

Paz es ofrecerle a alguien tu mano.

Peace is the words you say to a brother.

Paz son las palabras dichas a un hermano.

Will you stay with me?
Will you be my friend?
Will you listen to my story
 till the very end?

¿Te quedarás a mi lado?
¿Querrás ser mi amigo?
¿Escucharás el cuento
hasta el final conmigo?

Will you wait when I'm slow?
Will you calm my fears?
Will you sing to the sun
to dry my tears?

¿Esperarás por mí?
¿Mis miedos calmarás?
¿Le pedirás al sol
mis lágrimas secar?

Will you keep me company when I'm all alone?
Will you give me shelter when I've lost my home?

¿Si me encuentro solo, me acompañarás?
¿Me darás refugio si pierdo mi hogar?

You might find peace in a photograph,

Encontrarás paz en esa foto hallada,

Or in the deep boom of a belly laugh.

o en el estallido de una carcajada.

And even in the wake of tragedy,
Even then, you might find her.
In the rubble of a fallen tower.
In the sorrow of your darkest hour.
In the hat of a hero.
In the loss of a friend.

E incluso ante una tragedia,
serás capaz de encontrarla.
En los escombros de una torre caída.
En los peores momentos de tu vida.
En el sombrero de un héroe.
Cuando un amigo ya no está.

Peace is a joining, not a pulling apart.
It's the courage to bear a wounded heart.

La paz es unir, nunca desunir.
Con el alma herida poder resistir.

It's a safe place to live.
It's the freedom from fear.

Es un lugar seguro para vivir.
Es vivir sin tener miedos en la vida.

It's a kiss or a hug
When you've lost someone dear.

Es un beso o un abrazo
por la pérdida sufrida.

So offer a cookie,

Ofrece una galleta,

Walk away from a fight.

las peleas rehúsa.

Comfort a friend
Through the long, dark night.

Consuela a un amigo
en la noche oscura.

Sing a quiet song.

Canta una suave canción.

Catch a falling star.

Toma una estrella fugaz.

May peace walk beside you
Wherever you are.

Que la paz esté contigo
allí donde tú estás.